INSIDE THIS

BOOK

(are
three
books).

**by Barney
Saltzberg**

Abrams Appleseed

New York

Inside this book is a book I made, called . . .

My name is Seymour.

My mom made us books with blank pages.

I filled mine with drawings
of things I saw...

and things I heard...

feelings I had...

and stories I made up.

My sister, Fiona, made a book called . . .

INSIDE this ♥ BOOK, TOO!!
by Fiona

I'm an
ARTiST
and a
POET.

YES,
that's ME.

My book is
filled with
POETRY!

I PLAY with WORDS all the time.

A wagging tail
And a cold wet nose,
This is how
My morning goes.
I know that when
He gets this way...
Our dog, Fleabee,
Wants to play!

I could write poems from here to the **MOON.**

The only trouble is...

Then our little brother, Wilbur, made his book. He can't write yet, so he drew pictures and told me what to write.

MY BOOK

by Wilbur

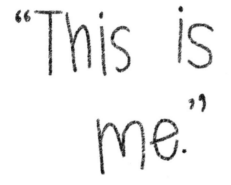

"This i

We read our
books over and
over and over,
and decided to
put each one . . .

Inside this book!